Goblins
& Ghosties

This paperback edition published 2016
First published 2015 by Bloomsbury Publishing Plc
50 Bedford Square, London, WC1B 3DP

www.bloomsbury.com

Bloomsbury is a registered trademark of Bloomsbury Publishing Plc

Copyright © Bloomsbury Publishing Plc 2015
Text copyright © Maggie Pearson 2015
Illustrations © Francesca Greenwood 2015

The moral rights of the author have been asserted.

ISBN 978-1-4729-1369-2

A CIP catalogue for this book is available from the British Library.

Printed and bound by CPI Group (UK) Ltd, Croydon CR0 4YY

FSC
www.fsc.org

MIX
Paper from
responsible sources
FSC® C020471

1 3 5 7 9 10 8 6 4 2

STORIES OF DARKNESS
FROM AROUND THE WORLD

Goblins
& Ghosties

MAGGIE PEARSON

Illustrated by
Francesca Greenwood

BLOOMSBURY EDUCATION
AN IMPRINT OF BLOOMSBURY
LONDON OXFORD NEW YORK NEW DELHI SYDNEY

From goblins and ghosties and long-leggitty beasties
And things that go bump in the night,
Good Lord, protect us!

Contents

The Moddey-dhoo
Isle of Man

It was a dark and stormy winter's night. Peel Castle was deserted, apart from the three soldiers and their sergeant who'd been left on watch. There they sat, huddling round the fire in the guardhouse, when in walked a great black dog.

'How did that animal get in?' roared the sergeant. 'Which one of you left the gate open?'

The other three shook their heads.

'It wasn't me.'

'Nor me, sarge.'

'Nor me neither.'

'Hang on a minute,' said the first man. 'We're on an island. How did the dog get across?'

'It must have swum,' said the second.

'So how come it's as dry as a bone?'

The third one said nothing.

All four of them stood and stared at the dog. The dog stared back for a bit. Then, it sauntered over to the snuggest, warmest place by the fire and lay down with its chin on its paws, watching them.

The size of it! Big as a moorland pony, it was, with feet the size of tea plates and eyes like red-rimmed saucers.

At last the third soldier found his voice. 'That's no dog we've got there. I reckon that's the Moddey-dhoo.'

'I've heard of it,' the second man said. 'You see the Moddey-dhoo, that means death!'

That's not what I heard,' said the first man. 'The way I heard it, there was this fisherman on his way to work who found his way blocked by the Moddey-dhoo and had to go home again. The boat he should have been on was lost with all hands.'

'There you are, then. Death!'

'Not for the man who saw it.'

'What you're saying is, we're all right then?'

'What I'm saying,' said the sergeant, 'is if we don't bother it, it won't bother us. Right?'

They tried to go on as if the dog wasn't there, chatting and playing cards, but of course it was there and though every time they looked it seemed to be asleep, they couldn't get over the feeling that it was watching them.

Whenever the duty man got up, took the keys and went to the door to go on his rounds, the dog was there at his heels.

So one of the others went with him, to keep one eye on his comrade, the other on the Moddey-dhoo.

All three of them came back safe and sound. No problem.

At first light the dog got up, strolled to the door and disappeared. Not a whisker of it was to be seen up and down the corridor outside.

But, the next night, it was back again. And the night after that. It didn't come every night but often enough that the soldiers got into the habit of going round in pairs, just in case they met the Moddey-dhoo on the way.

Then, one of the four got transferred to another posting. A mainlander took his place. A Londoner they called Mad Jack.

Mad Jack just laughed when they warned him about the Moddey-dhoo.

'You're having me on!' he said. 'It's just a big, black dog, right? I'm good with dogs. Where are you, Moddey-doody-dhoo? Here, boy! Come!'

Suddenly, the dog was there in the doorway, fixing Mad Jack with its red-rimmed eyes, padding past him on its paws the size of tea plates to its favourite spot by the fire.

'Like I said,' laughed Jack. 'It's just a dog.'

The time came for the duty man to go on his rounds. 'I'll go!' said Mad Jack. 'No need to come with me. Old Moddey-dhoo will keep me company. Come on, boy. Walkies!'

Straightaway, the dog was on its feet and

at Mad Jack's heels as he swaggered out of the room. Following so close that it might have been his shadow.

The other three men sat listening, as the sound of Mad Jack's footsteps and the jangling of the keys faded into the distance.

Silence. Long enough for a man to count to ten, very slowly, but then broken by a terrible, blood-curdling scream.

And silence again, until the first light of morning when the three men crept out to see what had happened to Mad Jack and the Moddey-dhoo.

Although they searched the castle from top to bottom, they found not one trace of either.

Note: In the old Manx language Moddey-dhoo would be pronounced moor-tha-doo.

The Bride Who Waited
Native American

She was a maiden of the Brule Sioux and he was a wandering white man.

The tribe didn't care much for white men in general, but this one was quietly spoken. He respected their ways and knew their language, so they welcomed him into their camp.

All that summer he lived as one of the tribe, hunting with the men by day and in the evening, when the whole tribe gathered round the camp fire, he told them tales of the places he'd been.

The things he'd seen! He told them about the Californian goldfields where a man could make enough in a day to keep him in comfort for the rest of his life. And the Mississippi river boats where he could lose it all at the gambling tables just as fast. He described the cities of the east, with buildings towering up taller than the tallest tree and so brightly lit by night that the stars hid their light for shame.

Always as he talked his eyes seemed to seek her out, as if he were telling these stories just for her.

'Marry me,' he whispered, 'and I'll take you there.'

'You must speak to my father,' she said.

So he spoke to her father, who consulted the tribal elders, who all agreed that it might not be such a bad thing, in view of the way the world was changing, to have a member of the tribe living in the white man's world, learning their ways, their customs.

So the white man and the Sioux maiden were married.

'When will you take me there?' she asked him. 'When will you take me to this brave new world of yours?'

'Just as soon as I've found a place for us to live,' he promised. 'Will you wait for me?'

'You know I will. I am your wife. However long it takes, you'll find me here, waiting.'

So off he went.

Summer ended. The tribe was packing up, moving south to their winter camp.

'I must stay here,' she said, 'and wait for my husband.'

So they left her there with a stash of food and fuel to see her through the winter.

All the long winter she waited but he didn't come.

He'd scarcely ridden a few days from the summer camp when the wanderlust took hold of him again. It would be good, he thought, to ride the Mississippi river boats one last time, maybe double his money at the gambling tables, so he could buy a better house.

Maybe not. Soon, he'd not one red cent to his name. Nothing for it but to try his luck in the California gold fields. When that didn't pan out, he headed east again, joining a cattle drive, though that didn't pay more than enough to keep body and soul together along the way. Nothing left over for setting up house with his pretty little Indian bride.

She'd promised to wait for him, but how long was it now that he'd been gone?

Too long, he told himself, looking in the mirror one day as he shaved, seeing the grey threads in his hair among the brown. She'll have forgotten me by now.

Still, more and more she haunted his dreams. Sometimes, he seemed to hear her voice calling him, no more than a whispering in the wind. Sometimes, among the bustling crowds, he'd see her standing, holding out her arms to him.

So one day he turned westward, seeking the place, never expecting to find it again – but glory be! There it was. A lone tipi standing in the midst of that vast empty plain, looking as fresh and new as it did on their wedding night.

And there in the doorway was his Indian

bride, not a grey hair on her head among the raven black. 'You stayed away too long,' she said. And the sound of her voice was soft as the wind rustling through long grass. 'I know,' he said. 'And I'm truly sorry.'

The scent of her skin when he took her in his arms was as sweet as summer rain.

'This time,' she whispered, 'I'm never going to let you go.'

It was a party of homesteaders heading west that found them, not long after. A white man lying stone dead under the ragged remains of an old tipi, holding in his arms a bundle of sun-bleached bones and a strand of raven-black hair twined in his fingers.

The Vampire
of Croglin Grange
England

It was the perfect place for a summer holiday, an old manor house set among wooded valleys and rolling moors where they could walk all day and never see another human soul.

'And in the evenings,' said Amelia, 'we'll tell each other ghost stories by candlelight. Croglin Grange! It does sound so wonderfully gothic!'

There was even an old chapel in the grounds. Sadly, the door was shut.

'Never mind,' she said. 'We can ask in the village. Somebody must have a key.'

'How did you manage to rent the place so cheaply?' Edward asked their brother.

'Well, I'm afraid there's no electricity and no servants,' said Michael.

'That doesn't matter!' said Edward. 'We can fend for ourselves. Cook our own food, come and go as we like. Without servants hovering around, looking all disapproving, we can do as we please.'

Next morning, the brothers were up bright and early, all set for a day exploring the moors.

Amelia hadn't slept a wink. 'I couldn't sleep for the sound of the rain rattling against my window.'

The boys looked puzzled.

'It didn't rain last night,' said Edward. 'The ground's as dry as a bone.'

Amelia yawned. 'Then it must have been a branch blown by the wind. Tap-tap-tap! All night long.'

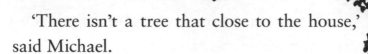

'There isn't a tree that close to the house,' said Michael.

'Perhaps it was mice you heard?' said Edward, grinning.

'Perhaps it was.' Amelia grinned back. She wasn't the sort of girl to be frightened by mice.

The next night she was woken by the same tap-tapping on the window.

That is definitely not mice, she thought. And if it isn't rain either, and it isn't a branch, well, the only way to find out what it is, is to go and look.

So up she got and went to the window, pulled back the curtain and looked out. Staring back at her was a hideous face!

Amelia screamed so loudly that her brothers came running.

'There's a man out there,' she said, 'looking in at the window!'

But, when the brothers pulled back the curtain...

'There's nobody there,' said Edward.

'How could there be?' said Michael. 'We're on the first floor and there's no way anyone could climb up.'

'It must have been your own reflection you saw,' they said. 'Either that, or you were still half asleep and dreaming.'

Amelia knew it wasn't her own reflection she'd seen. And that she'd been wide awake when she saw it.

The next night, instead of going to bed, she sat up in a chair, waiting.

Sure enough – tap, tap, tap came at the window.

She drew back the curtain and there was the same man's face staring back.

This time, being ready, she decided it wasn't such a scary face after all. In fact, he was quite handsome.

'Who are you?' she asked him. 'And how did you get up there?'

'Let me in, Amelia,' he said, 'and I'll tell you.'

'How do you know my name?' she asked him.

'I'll tell you that, too,' he said. 'But it's hard trying to talk with the window between us. Won't you please open it, Amelia dear?'

So she opened the window.

'I'm still waiting for you to invite me in,' the stranger said.

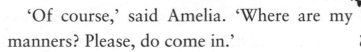

'Of course,' said Amelia. 'Where are my manners? Please, do come in.'

'Take my hand, then, and help me.'

So she took hold of his hand to help him. And the touch of that hand was as cold as death.

He smiled at the shocked look on her face. She saw his teeth, like fangs, and they were stained with blood.

Suddenly she was very, very afraid: too afraid even to scream.

So maybe it was the draught of cold air from the open window that woke her brothers, or maybe it was some sixth sense that told them their sister was in deadly danger, but just in the nick of time they burst in at the door. Together, they fought off the intruder until he fled, half-running, half-flying – so it seemed – like a wounded bat, towards the old chapel where they lost sight of him.

The brothers went down there at once, but found the place locked tight, just as it had been before. First thing next morning they fetched the vicar, who brought the key. After him flocked the villagers, who'd all heard tales from their grandparents' time of strange goings-on up at the grange. Not the sort of tales that you shared with townies, of course, when they turned up for the summer with money to spend.

At first sight, when the door of the church was opened, everything looked just as it should, apart from one tomb whose lid was slightly askew.

'Lift it off!' said the vicar.

Inside, staring up at them with red-rimmed eyes, lay the body of Amelia's night visitor, his fangs bared in a hideous grin. The corpse was as fresh as on the day when it had been laid to rest more than a hundred years before, if the inscription on the tomb was to be believed.

Under the vicar's instructions, the villagers took the body, chopped off the head and burnt it along with the rest. They scattered the ashes to the four winds and that, it seems, was the end of the Croglin Grange vampire.

But Amelia never got back the use of her right arm, in spite of all that the doctors could do. It was as if the arm were dead. And cold, so cold! As cold as the vampire's touch.

Hold Him, Tubbs!
Southern United States

There were three of us in those days, John-Henry and me and Tubbs. I don't rightly know why we called him Tubbs. It wasn't his family name and no way would you have said he was tubby. Tubbs was small and skinny – but a fighter! Many's the time John-Henry and me had earned us the price of a meal and a bed for the night by betting on Tubbs when he got into a scrap.

'Hold him, Tubbs!' we'd yell, as soon as he

got the other guy in a bear hug. 'Now you've got him!' (This being generally more of a no-holds-barred sort of wrestling match than a regular fist-fight.) Next thing, Tubbs would hook his leg round and the other guy would be flat on his back in the dust. Game over.

Most of the time, we just travelled around, looking for any sort of work, wherever we could find it. We didn't look too hard, just for enough to pay for a meal or two and a roof over our heads come nightfall.

Came the day when our luck ran out. We were miles from anywhere, no sign of shelter. Night was coming on, the rain was drizzling down and we could see it was going to get a whole lot worse before it got better. Then, we came upon this old plantation house. No one living there, that was plain to see from the creepers growing up the walls, the broken windows and the shutters hanging off their hinges.

'This'll do us for the night, I reckon,' said John-Henry.

'Reckon it will,' I said. 'Ain't no one around to tell us we can't.'

That's where I was wrong. Lord knows how long he'd been watching us, dressed all in black from his hat to his boots, sitting there so still on his great black horse. Night coming on and no moon to see by, we'd never have noticed him if he hadn't spoken.

'Ain't no-one been living in that old house since way back,' he said. 'Ain't no one around here who'd stay in that house so much as one hour after nightfall and expect to come out alive.'

'Why's that?' said Tubbs.

'Because of the spook,' said the man. 'I'm just warning you, friendly like. You stay away.' He turned his horse and rode away before we could ask him if there was any place nearby where we could beg a bed for the night and a bite to eat in exchange for a hand's turn of work in the morning.

'Spook!' said Tubbs. 'You believe that stuff? He was just trying to scare us off.'

'All the same,' said John-Henry, 'maybe we'd better not risk it.'

'We can shelter out here under the trees just as good,' I said.

'Rain's coming on harder,' said Tubbs. 'I want a solid roof over my head tonight.'

He went on up to the house. Soon we could see, by the flickering light, that he'd lit a fire in the old fireplace. We could tell by the smell he was cooking himself a bite to eat.

'Sure you won't join me?' he called.

'No, no, we're fine out of here,' we shouted back – though we weren't. Nothing but damp wood lying around, so we couldn't get a fire to light. Nothing to eat but cold beans and stale bread. No place dry enough for us to catch a wink of sleep. The rain was soon coming down so hard, we might as well have been sitting under a waterfall for all the shelter the trees gave.

I thought of Tubbs settling down to sleep, snug as a bug in a rug. Even thought of joining him once or twice.

Glad I didn't.

Must have been around midnight, came this mighty clap of thunder. Lightning flashed, brighter than daylight.

Soon as my eyes stopped seeing fireworks, I could see there was something there in the room with Tubbs. That thing was blacker than black, like looking into a deep, dark, bottomless hole. It loomed over Tubbs lying there on the floor. Its voice, when it spoke, fair set my insides churning.

'Do you know who I am?' it said.

'Reckon you must be the spook we was told about,' said Tubbs. 'I'm Tubbs. Now we're acquainted, I'd be obliged if you'll leave me to get my beauty sleep.' He turned over and closed his eyes.

'Hey!' said the spook. 'I haven't finished with you yet.'

Tubbs opened his eyes. He stood up, very slowly, like a spring uncoiling. 'That sounds to me like fighting talk,' said Tubbs. He stood there, squaring up to that spook, all five foot four of him.

'My money's on Tubbs,' said John-Henry. 'What do you think?'

'I don't know,' I said. 'I never saw him wrestle a spook before.'

'He's got to go straight for the bear hug,' said John-Henry, 'before that spook knows what's hit him. Go for it, Tubbs!'

'You can take him!' I yelled.

As soon as the fight got started, I could see old Tubbs was in trouble.

That spook was more like smoke than solid flesh and blood. Every time Tubbs got his arms around it, the spook would just kind of dissolve into nothing, then pop up again behind him. But its fists were rock-hard solid. Time and again we saw old Tubbs go flying through the air and hit the wall, then pick himself up and come back fighting.

John-Henry and me, we kept on yelling encouragement.

'Go for him, Tubbs!'

'Look out! He's behind you.'

I could see old Tubbs was tiring, but he wasn't about to give up. Seemed like the spook was tiring too. Next time Tubbs got him in that bear hug, the spook didn't turn to smoke. It hugged old Tubbs right back. Like two lovers dancing, they went waltzing round the room.

'Now you've got him, Tubbs!' roared John-Henry.

'Hold him, Tubbs!' I yelled. 'Don't let him go!'

'I won't!' the spook roared back.

It shot up in the air taking Tubbs with it, straight through the ceiling, so fast that we both thought we'd see them shoot through the roof any second.

But we didn't.

We listened for sounds of the fight going on up above, but there was nothing. That house was silent as the grave.

'You think we should go look for him?' said John-Henry.

'Let's leave it till morning,' I said.

Soon as it was light, we checked out that house from top to bottom, opening cupboards, knocking on walls, calling out, 'Tubbs! Are you there?'

Nothing.

'Looks like old Tubbs is gone for good,' said John-Henry.

I shook my head. 'He'll be back,' I said. 'Just as soon as he's licked that spook.'

That must be some fight they're having in Spookland, though. We ain't seen hide nor hair of old Tubbs from that day to this.

The Grateful Dead
Gypsy

There was once a gypsy who'd grown tired of the travelling life and decided it was time to settle down. He'd saved enough money over the years to set himself up in business, in a small way. A shop, maybe, since buying and selling was what he'd always been good at.

The question was, what sort of shop? And in which town or village? None of the places he'd passed through on his travels seemed exactly right, but the gypsy was a great believer in Fate. Fate would bring him to the place where he was supposed to be after all his years of travelling and he'd know it the moment he saw it. Meanwhile, he kept travelling on.

One day, as he was passing a graveyard, he heard a man shouting at the top of his voice, 'Give me back my money, you dirty gypsy!'

The gypsy looked around, surprised. He'd never owed anyone money in his life.

But it wasn't him the man was shouting at.

The man was kicking at a newly covered grave. 'Come out!' he yelled. 'And give me my money!'

'Peace, friend,' said the gypsy. 'Let the dead rest in peace.'

'Would you?' said the man, 'if you were in my shoes? This cheating gypsy borrowed money from me. If he thinks he can get out of paying me by burying himself six feet under, he's got another think coming.'

'I'll pay his debt,' said the gypsy. 'How much did he owe you?'

The sum the man said he was owed turned

about to be nearly half the money the gypsy had put by, but the gypsy didn't argue. He paid the man, then lingered a while by the grave so that he wouldn't have to walk on into town with this odious fellow for company.

Dusk was falling by the time he took to the road again.

He found there was someone walking beside him, keeping pace with him, step by step. How long the man had been there was hard to say, since the sun had set and the moon was not yet risen. The stranger walked so softly, it might have been no more than the gypsy's own shadow. The gypsy asked the stranger, 'How far is it to the town? Do you know?'

And the stranger answered him, 'It's just over this next hill. I lived there for a while, but then – you'd understand, being a travelling man yourself – sometimes the urge to move on becomes too strong.'

'Still, I'm thinking it's time I settled down,' said the gypsy. 'I've money saved and a pretty good head for business...'

'Ah! That's what I don't have,' said the

stranger. 'I trained as a butcher – none better, if I do say it myself – but as to the buying and selling and keeping the books straight…'

'I'm a great believer in Fate,' said the gypsy. 'I'd say it was Fate that threw us together.'

To cut a long story short, the two of them set up a butchery business together in that very same town. The gypsy did the buying and selling and his new partner worked behind the scenes, slaughtering, butchering, jointing, slicing and mincing, curing hams and making sausages, patés and pies. Word soon got about that this was the best butcher's shop for miles around.

There was just one thing that always seemed to be sold out, though the gypsy never saw the going of it. No matter how many times he was asked for liver, there was never any in the storeroom when he went to look.

In the end he asked his partner, 'What has happened to all the liver again?'

The butcher said simply, 'I ate it.'

'Oh. All of it?'

'I'm sorry. I need it, you see, for the blood.'

Now the gypsy came to look at him, he did always look a bit peaky.

'You should get out more,' he said. 'Fresh air and sunshine is what you need.'

But he could hardly tell his partner not to eat the liver, since the man took no share of the profits they were making.

'Why should I?' he said, 'I put no money into the business. What right have I to take money out? What do I need money for anyway? I have all I need.'

'A house would be nice, though, wouldn't it? And a few home comforts. You don't have to sleep in that draughty old lean-to out the back.'

The other man smiled. 'Settling down is one thing. Four solid walls and a roof above me might feel a bit too much like being buried alive. But if you've got the money to spare, I think it's time we took on an apprentice.'

So a boy was found and the butcher trained him up till he declared that the boy knew everything he could teach him. 'So now I must be on my way,' he said.

'Must you go?' said his friend.

'It's time,' said the butcher. 'I'm afraid I must.'

'Is it the old travelling urge?'

'Something like that. Will you walk with me part of the way along the road?'

Seeing he wasn't about to change his mind, the gypsy fell into step beside him.

'I thought we were friends,' he said.

'So we are.'

'Then why are you going?'

'Because I must.'

'Is it my fault? Is it something I've done? I've offered you a share of the business.'

The butcher smiled and shook his head. 'You've done all that a friend can do – and more, even when we were strangers. You remember this place?' he said, stopping at the gate of the graveyard. 'This is where we first met.'

'I remember some oaf trying to get money from a dead man.'

'Let the dead rest in peace, you said. You paid my debt, though I was a stranger to you then. Now I've repaid you in full. And now I shall rest in peace.'

He walked away into the gathering darkness.

The Man of Her Dreams
Nigeria

Every parent thinks, in fact they know, that their baby is the prettiest baby that ever was born. And the most remarkable!

It's true, Ogilisa was a very pretty baby and she grew into an even prettier little girl, with big brown eyes and perfect teeth, smooth skin and a glorious mop of hair. But the only really remarkable thing about her was that she was remarkably spoilt.

Whatever Ogilisa wanted, she got, whether it was toys to play with, dresses to wear or beads to thread in her hair. If she decided she wanted to eat nothing but ice cream for a week, ice cream was what she got.

As for helping, just a little bit, around the house? She fell into such a tantrum when her mother suggested it, that it was never mentioned again.

Ogilisa had better things to do, like giving her playmates merry hell when they didn't do exactly as she wanted them to, and sitting in front of the mirror making herself even more beautiful, so she'd be ready when the man of her dreams came along.

None of the young men in the village would do. The only use Ogilisa had for them was to make fun of them.

Zeke had the most beautiful hair, it was true, but he was so tall and thin, he could hire himself out as a beanpole. Moses had beautiful eyes – but his ears! She'd have to peg him down whenever the wind blew to stop him being carried away. Sunny had fine long, strong legs, but his hands were like two bunches of bananas. Whereas Victor had fine, delicate hands, but his mouth was so wide – like a frog! When his children were born, they'd probably turn out to be tadpoles. Ade's voice was divine – so long as you kept your eyes shut – for he had a face like a baboon!

All her friends giggled along and laughed behind their hands when any of the young men happened by. Secretly, Ogilisa's friends wouldn't have minded if any young man had thrown one of them more than a passing glance. But the only girl that the young men ever had eyes for was Ogilisa.

'So what is he like, the man of your dreams?' the other girls wanted to know. Maybe if they could find her someone, anyone, who measured up, then she'd be out of their hair.

'Well,' said Ogilisa, thoughtfully, 'he's got hair like Zeke's and eyes like Moses'. He has fine strong legs like Sunny's, but his hands are slim and delicate like Victor's. His voice is soft and warm, like Ade's...'

Be careful what you wish for! You never

know who might be listening.

A mischievous spirit heard Ogilisa, and thought it was time she was taught a lesson.

But spirits are nothing but air and shadows. What was he to do for a body? Borrow one, that's what. Patch it together from the bits of the young men that Ogilisa most admired.

A little while later Moses felt strangely tired. He crawled into a patch of bushes where he fell asleep and dreamed he was wandering in the pitch dark. Meanwhile that mischievous spirit went on its way seeing the world through Moses' borrowed eyes.

Zeke's mother kept calling him to come and help with the chores. It was lucky she just gave up and didn't go into his room to wake him. What would she have said if she'd seen he'd suddenly lost all his hair?

One by one the young men Ogilisa had named fell into a deep, deep sleep, while that mischievous spirit ran round, cherry-picking the best bits of them, until he'd put himself together in the shape of the man of Ogilisa's dreams. Lastly he stole Ade's voice.

It was Ade's voice that Ogilisa heard talking to her mother at the door. What did that baboon-face want? She hid herself behind a curtain and peeped out, but it wasn't Ade's face that she saw. It was the man of her dreams! Face, hair, eyes, hands, legs and all the rest. Everything about him was just perfect.

'Beautiful Ogilisa!' he said. 'I've travelled from far away to see if you're as beautiful as they say. Now, I see you are. Will you marry me? I warn you, if you say yes, it has to be this very day.'

'Yes! Yes! Yes!' cried Ogilisa. 'Mama! Papa! Send for the priest. I'm getting married this very day.'

The priest came, muttering that this was all most irregular, caught a steely look from the bride and decided on a quiet life.

The whole village – almost – turned out to see Ogilisa married.

But, as everyone else sat down for the wedding feast, the bridegroom said, 'Now, we have to be on our way.' The sun was going down and he knew his magic wouldn't last beyond nightfall.

'Where are we going?' said Ogilisa.

'You'll see when we get there.'

That wasn't good enough for Ogilisa. But when she turned to argue, all she could find to say was, 'What happened to your hair?'

The spirit ran a hand over his bald head. Zeke must have woken early.

'There's no time to explain,' he said. 'Come on, Ogilisa. We must hurry.'

As the sun dipped below the horizon, Moses was waking, opening his eyes, and looking about. 'Help me, Ogilisa,' said the spirit. 'I can't see the road.'

'It's there in front of us. What's the matter with you?'

'Just take my hand and lead me along it.'

'Where is your hand? I can't feel it.'

'Ah! Victor must have woken,' he said sadly. 'Sunny too. I'm sorry, Ogilisa. I can't go a step further.'

'Where are you?'

'Down here.'

'What happened to your legs?'

'Gone.'

Wasn't that Ade's voice? Hadn't it always been Ade's voice she heard, whenever her husband spoke?

'Ade? Is that you? Where are you? If this is a joke, it's not very funny. Where is my husband?'

'I'm here, Ogilisa. Right beside you.'

'Where? Where?' Ogilisa turned round and about. 'Stop playing games! I'm frightened.'

The spirit felt sorry for her. He would have liked to explain. But at that moment Ade, too, woke up and recovered his voice.

And she was left all alone in the dark.

Little Olle and The Troll
Sweden

Everyone was pretty sure there must be a troll lurking in the woods around the village, because so many animals had gone missing lately. A pig here, a goose there, even a cow and her calf. It all added up to one thing.

'So what does he look like, this troll?' demanded Olle. 'How will I know him if I see him?'

'You'll know him, all right!'

'But how?'

The villagers looked at one another. What did a troll look like? The truth was, none of them had ever seen one, but they weren't going to admit they didn't know, not to little Olle.

'Well, for a start, he's big and hairy!'

'He has a nose like a pig's snout... and tusks, like a wild boar!'

'His eyes are red...'

' ... and his teeth are green...'

'... and one of his feet has a cloven hoof, like a goat.'

Talking of goats, the very next morning when Olle's mother went out to milk their goat, it had gone!

'Better the goat than you, Olle,' she said. 'For what trolls like best to eat is a nice, plump, healthy boy. So lock the door when I've gone and don't open it till I come back from market.'

The troll watched patiently till she was

out of sight, then he ambled out of the forest where he'd been hiding close by. That troll was hungry. He'd got the goat hidden away for when he felt peckish later, but just at the moment what he really fancied was a nice, plump, juicy boy.

He knocked on the door of the cottage.

'Who's that?' called Olle.

'I'm a poor, weary traveller,' the troll called back, 'looking for a place to rest. Can I come in, please?'

'Sorry,' said Olle. 'I'm not allowed to open the door till Mama gets back, because of the troll.'

'Do I look like a troll?' The troll ambled round to the window so Olle could see him. He was big and hairy, but so, too, were a few of the men from the village that Olle could name. And he didn't have red eyes or green teeth, or a nose like a pig's, or tusks, or even a cloven hoof for a foot as far as Olle could see.

'Can I come in now, please?' said the troll.

'Sorry,' said Olle, 'but Mama was very firm. We know the troll can't be far away because he stole our goat last night.'

'Why do trolls always get the blame?' said the troll. 'How do you know she hasn't just wandered off? As a matter of fact,' he added, 'I saw a goat grazing all on her own as I was coming along. I don't know if it was your goat. You'd be able to tell me. Come with me and I'll show you the place. With any luck she'll still be there.'

'I can't come out,' said Olle. 'Mama told me not to open the door.'

'You could climb out of the window,' said the troll. 'Think how pleased your mum will be when she comes home and finds the goat, safe and sound.'

Olle thought about it.

He opened the window.

'Come on, then,' said the troll. 'Out you come!'

'Wait a minute,' said Olle. 'Is it far?'

'Far-ish,' said the troll.

Then I'd better bring something to eat on the way.' Quickly Olle wrapped up a piece of honey cake and stuffed it in his pocket.

Then, with the troll's help, he climbed out of the window and off they went, down the path and deep into the forest.

If you're wondering why the troll didn't grab little Olle and gobble him up on the spot, well, maybe he was getting to an age where he didn't like to rush his meals and risk getting indigestion. Maybe he liked the idea of having his dinner walk to his lair on its own two legs instead of being carried kicking and screaming. Maybe he was actually enjoying having little Olle trotting along beside him, chatting away about nothing in particular, since trolls, on the whole, don't have many friends.

Whatever. They walked along till Olle got tired. Then they sat down for a rest. Olle got out the honey cake and offered the troll a piece.

The troll shook his head. 'My mum says it'll spoil my dinner.'

'That's what my mama says too!' said Olle. Then, at the thought of this big ugly man having a mum who still told him what to do, he started to laugh.

Olle had one of those laughs that are catching. Soon the troll was laughing too. His mouth opened wide and Olle couldn't resist it. He tossed in a piece of honey cake.

The troll coughed and spluttered. He did everything he could not to swallow that piece of cake, but down it went.

Say what you will about trolls, but they do have certain standards. If somebody gives them a present, they don't feel it's right to eat that person until they've given something back.

Will he, nil he, the troll had eaten a piece of Olle's honey cake. What did the troll have to give little Olle?

Only the goat he'd stolen the night before.

Tripping down the hillside she came, as soon as the troll whistled.

'I told you she'd just wandered off,' said the troll.

'Thank you! Thank you!' cried Olle. He threw his arms round the troll's neck and gave him a big kiss on his ugly face. 'Mama will be so pleased.'

Off he trotted, home again, leading the goat behind him. The troll stood rubbing his hairy cheek where Little Olle had kissed him, wondering why he hadn't grabbed that plump, juicy boy and eaten him, the minute he'd given the goat back.

Ah, well, maybe next time...

Wungala
Australia

Wungala went out gathering food one day, taking her little boy, Bulla, with her. He was a good kid, bright as a button and chirpy as a cricket. It always made the day go faster, having him with her. Before she knew it, the sun was sliding down the sky.

Might as well eat before we go home, she thought.

So she sat down in the shade of a coolabah tree beside a water hole. She lit a cooking fire.

Then, she found herself a big flat stone and started grinding away at some of the seeds she'd gathered, grinding them into flour to make damper bread.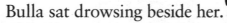

Bulla sat drowsing beside her.

Suddenly he sat bolt upright, 'Who's that, Ma?'

Wungala had to screw up her eyes against the dying sun to see where he was pointing. All she could see was a figure standing outlined against the sky.

'Him?' she said. 'He's just a man.'

She went on grinding the flour to make damper bread. All the same she was starting to have a bad feeling about that man she'd seen.

'He's watching us, Ma.'

'He can watch if he wants. He might even learn something.'

While she was stoking up the fire to get the ashes nice and hot so she could cook the damper bread, she snatched another look.

That was no mortal man.

Once or twice, when Bulla was really bad,

she'd said to him, 'If you don't behave yourself that old wulgaru will come and get you!' Same as her mother used to say to her, just something you say to bring the kid into line, always believing it was all moonshine. Now, there he was, large as life and twice as ugly. The wulgaru.

The story was, as far as she could remember, that there was once a man, Djarapa. A lazy beggar, he was, but smart. Maybe that was his trouble, so busy thinking of all the smart stuff he was going to do that he never got round to actually doing anything. Then, one day, he hit on the idea of building himself a slave to do all the work for him, so he could spend all the time doing his smart thinking.

So the wulgaru was born, out of odd bits of wood and stone and clay with magic songs to give him life. But it wasn't long before the two of them fell out, maybe because the wulgaru didn't take kindly to doing all the work while Djarapa sat on his backside. The wulgaru took off into the bush and Djarapa couldn't be bothered to go after him.

Now the wulgaru haunts the faraway, silent places. They do say he eats people, when he can get them. Kids, mainly, who are too small to fight back, because deep down inside he's a coward. So mostly he sticks to frightening people. If you show him you're not frightened, that kind of unsettles him. Enough to give you a chance of making a run for it, anyway.

So Wungala went on calmly grinding the seeds into flour and when she'd done that she sent Bulla down to the water hole – 'But stay this side of it, you hear me?' – to fetch some water to mix with the flour to make the damper bread.

When she'd made the dough with the water and flour, she pushed the bread into the hot ashes to cook.

'He's coming closer, Ma,' whispered Bulla. 'He was just the other side of the water hole when I went there. Now he's creeping round it, coming this way.'

'Let him come,' said Wungala. 'Maybe he's hungry. Maybe we should share with him. What do you think?'

'I think I should stick real close to you, Ma.'

'Good boy. You do that.'

By the time the damper bread was cooked, the wulgaru was crouching opposite them, just the other side of the fire, but still puzzled, wondering why they didn't seem frightened. Why didn't they scream and run?

Instead, Wungala smiled at him as she hooked the hot damper bread out of the fire. 'You want some, wulgaru?' she said. 'You want some? Come and get it, then.'

The wulgaru leaned closer, and Wungala, smiling all the time, tossed that hot slab of damper bread from hand to hand.

Boy, it smelt good!

'Closer,' she crooned. 'Come closer.'

The wulgaru leaned closer and closer, till he was within arm's reach. 'You want some? You can have it all!' cried Wungala.

She pushed the damper right into the wulgaru's face.

That damper was piping hot – and sticky too! The wulgaru couldn't breathe or see or even think straight. He howled and spun and danced and clawed at that stuff till he could breathe again.

Then he let out a great roar.

Still the damper bread clung and burned, while the wulgaru spun and hopped and danced, trying to claw it away from his eyes. Where was she, the woman who'd done this to him? Soon as he caught her, he'd tear her limb from limb – but first he'd gobble up that kid of hers, snip-snap, bones and all, right in front of her eyes!

Round and round he danced, looking all over for them, but Wungala and Bulla were long gone, racing all the way back to camp, leaving the wulgaru still spinning, dancing himself dizzy till he tumbled head first into the cool, cool water.

All this happened a long time ago, but the wulgaru hasn't forgotten. Nor has Wungala.

She never threatened Bulla with the wulgaru again. Even now, she's scared of speaking his name even in a whisper, just in case the wulgaru hears her.

Speak of the devil, they say, and he will appear.

The Dauntless Girl
Ireland

Good evening, sir, and what can I get you? A drink to keep out the cold? Coming right up. Yes, sir, it is quiet in here. Always is at this time, as soon as the evenings start drawing in. That's when the regulars start taking the long way round instead of the short cut through the graveyard. 'Why's that?' you ask. Well, you being an educated man and a townie, too, you probably don't believe in ghosts.

Our Molly was the same, though she was local, born and bred.

She was a grand girl, was Molly. A hard worker and cheerful with it. The one thing she wouldn't put up with was being idle.

Evenings like this she'd stand, hand on hip, fingers drumming on the bar. 'What's keeping them?' she'd say.

'You know what's keeping them,' I'd tell her. 'They're afraid to take the shortcut through the graveyard after dark.'

'Afraid of ghosts!' she would scoff. 'Afraid of their own shadows!'

Then, one night, she told the customers to their faces, 'You're scared, all of you. Aren't you? Look at you! Great big men, afraid to walk across the graveyard in the dark! Poor babies!'

I heard someone mutter something about it all being very well for her to talk, as she didn't have to do it.

'Alright, then,' said Molly. 'I will. This very minute!' She flung down the cloth she'd been using to wipe the glasses. 'I'll be there and back again before you've finished that pint. And if I do meet a dead man, risen from the grave, I'll have the shroud off him and bring it back as a souvenir.'

Out of the door she went, across the road and into the graveyard.

As to what happened next, all I can say for sure is that we waited for her to come back. There were so many men crowded round the windows, that I never got so much as a look. One or two of them swore they could see she'd stopped part way across and was talking to someone.

Next thing most of us knew, she was haring back towards us with some long, white thing trailing behind her, so they said. I just heard her yelling.

'Open the door!' she cried. 'Let me in!'

As soon as she was back inside and the door locked fast behind her, we saw that she'd been as good as her word. That long, white thing was a shroud, right enough. You could tell by the smell of it. Fair stank the place out with its graveyard smell.

Then, from outside, came a sound like bones rattling and a voice: dry, rasping and angry. 'Give it back, Molly. Give me back my shroud!' Then it was pleading: 'Give it back, Molly, I'm begging you. I'm naked without it and cold – so cold.'

I felt sorry for the poor creature. 'Give it back, Molly,' I said. 'Just hand it to him out of the window.'

Molly shook her head.

The ghost, ghoul, zombie – whatever it was – went on rattling and pleading.

'Go on, Molly,' I said. 'Go on.'

But she wouldn't.

So I took the shroud out of Molly's hand, opened the window and thrust it outside.

'Here, take it,' I said.

The creature wouldn't take it. 'I must have it back from her own hands,' it said.

'Here, Molly,' I said, offering her the shroud.

She didn't want to take it, but she saw the faces of the men standing round, the ones she'd called cowards and babies, all watching to see what she'd do. So she took the shroud from me and held it out of the window.

And, would you believe it, the creature still wouldn't take it. 'You have to hand it back in the same place where you took it from me,' it said.

Then it turned away and walked back across the churchyard, its naked bones rattling with cold every step of the way.

'Go on, Molly,' I said. 'You'll be doing him a kindness.'

'Go on,' they all said. 'Go on, or we'll be stuck here all night.'

'Go on, Molly. We're right behind you.'

So off went Molly with the shroud in her hand, while the rest of us stood and waited.

When she came back she was as pale as death. She walked straight past us without a word, went upstairs and took to her bed.

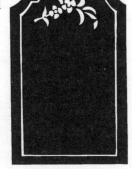

I never had time to call the doctor, for she was dead by morning.

We buried her there in the graveyard.

Now they do say there are two ghosts haunting the graveyard and I'd say that's very likely, for Molly never could stand being idle.

That's a good yarn, you say. But it's true, every word of it, sure as I'm standing here. If you wait a little longer, sir, the lads will be in soon. They'll back me up. Ah, well, if your friends are expecting you for dinner down in the village... if you take the shortcut through the graveyard opposite, you can be there in half the time. I wouldn't chance it myself, not at this time of night, but you being an educated man... I'll just stand here and keep an eye out till I see you're safely across.

The Ghost's Peso
Colombia

Juanita knew when she married Manuel that they were never going to be rich. He was smart enough to find work and he'd work hard till he'd earned enough to keep a roof over their heads and food on the table. Then, he'd take things easy for a bit. So there was never anything put by for a rainy day.

When that rainy day did come – as rainy days have a nasty habit of doing – and she lost her job cleaning up at the hacienda when the family shut up the house and moved to the city, they soon fell behind with the rent.

The manager left in charge of the estate was still hiring men, but at such poor wages! 'You pay peanuts,' said Manuel, 'you get monkeys. I'm nobody's monkey.'

But there was no other work around. Not men's work anyway.

Juanita did what she could: a bit of sewing, a bit of ironing, an evening dishwashing at the cantina. It was never enough. First Manuel borrowed money here, then a little more there so he could pay the first lot back and have enough left over to keep them going till pay-day. Soon he owed money here, there and everywhere.

Bit by bit they sold off everything they owned, till they were sleeping on the floor and eating nothing but watery soup straight out of the single cooking pot they'd got left. Still the creditors kept coming.

'If only we could pay them off,' said Juanita, 'we could move away from here. Start a new life.'

'There's only one way to stop them,' said Manuel. 'If I die, my debts die with me.'

'But I don't want you to die,' said Juanita.

'Nor do I,' said Manuel. 'But if they think I'm dead…'

'Ah!'

They sold the cooking pot to buy a coffin.

There lay Manuel in his coffin in the church, a single candle burning by his head. 'It was all we could afford!' sighed Juanita, the grieving widow, making all the creditors feel guilty. 'I know he died owing you money,' she told them. 'It was worrying about it that killed him. His heart, you know.'

'Oh, poor Manuel!' They shook their heads. 'If only we'd known!'

'Consider it paid.'

'The slate wiped clean.'

All except one. The sum Manuel owed him was tiny. Just one peso.

Juanita shook her head. 'I'm sorry,' she said. 'I haven't got it. I've nothing left in the world but that candle burning at the head of the coffin.'

'I'll have that then,' he said.

'You can have what's left of it in the morning,' she said. 'Tonight I need it. You wouldn't want me to watch over my poor husband's coffin in the dark?'

'I can wait,' he said. And settled himself down in a shadowy corner of the church.

Now if you think Manuel and Juanita were the only people having a hard time of it when the big estate was mothballed, you'd be wrong. Some people had turned to outright robbery. And, as luck would have it, a band of robbers were passing the church that dark night, looking for somewhere where they could see to divide up their loot.

Seeing a light burning in the church, in they went.

'Who's that?' cried Manuel, sitting bolt upright in his coffin.

The thieves nearly died of fright on the spot. They dropped the stolen money and fled.

The noise they made woke the creditor, who'd been dozing in his shadowy corner of the church. Seeing Manuel sitting up in his coffin, he yelled, 'I knew it! I knew you were faking, you cheat! You shyster! Playing dead just to save yourself from paying the one measly peso you owe me! Give it to me now, or I'll wake the whole village – all the people you borrowed from – and show them how you tricked them. Give me my peso!'

It was just that last bit that the robbers heard when they'd plucked up courage enough to come creeping back for their loot – after all, money is money and they'd gone to a lot of trouble to get it.

'Give me my peso!'

They looked at one another in horror. The ghosts inside the church must be dividing up the money. Who else, apart from the dead man they'd seen, would be in the church at this hour? And if each of those ghosts was only getting one peso, how many ghosts would that be?

'How many pesos did we steal?'

'Dozens, at least.'

'More like hundreds.'

One dead man walking

they could probably deal with between them, but a church full of ghosts? No way!

They took to their heels again and this time they didn't come back.

Meanwhile, Manuel tossed a peso from the pile on the floor to his creditor, and then added another for luck.

One hundred per cent interest! The creditor went on his way contented, never suspecting that he'd just helped Manuel and Juanita to a small fortune.

By morning they were long gone, well on their way to the big city. Juanita had the moneybag stashed away under her layers of shawl until she could safely invest it in a little business. A shop or a market stall, maybe even a small hotel. One thing she was sure of. From now on, she'd be the only one to handle the cash.

Jean-Loup
Canada

O ld Joachim was the foulest old man you ever could wish not to meet.

Foul-tempered, foul-mouthed and foul-smelling. But he was the only miller within a long day's ride, so he was never short of business.

Day and night the mill wheel turned – even on Sundays, when honest, God-fearing folk shut up shop for the day and went to church.

The only small pleasure Joachim got out

of life was from playing chess, though he had to play against himself, since none of his neighbours could stand being in the same room with him long enough to get to checkmate.

Late one night, he was sitting over the chessboard, puzzling over a problem he'd cut out of the newspaper (and maybe he would have solved it quicker if he hadn't already been halfway down the bottle on the table beside him) when a knock came at the door.

There stood a young trapper, almost as filthy as Joachim himself, his hair wild and long and his clothes of poorly cured buckskin reeking of some sort of animal scent. Still, any God-fearing soul would have asked him in, since there'd been signs of a marauding beast prowling the area: a sheep mauled here, a dead cow there. It wasn't safe these days to be out after dark.

Joachim was about to shut the door, when the stranger, looking past him at the chessboard said, 'Do you fancy a game?'

'You play chess?'

'Just a little.'

'Come on in!'

He turned out to be a pretty good player. Not so good that old Joachim didn't beat him three times in a row, which pleased the old man no end.

'What's your name?' said Joachim.

'Jean-Loup,' said the stranger.

Soon, word got around that old Joachim had taken on assistant who was as foul-smelling and foul-tempered as his boss. Not so foul-mouthed, maybe, but only because he didn't speak much. His was more a brooding sort of ill temper. The way he looked at you! Made you nervous of turning your back.

Still, he and Joachim got along pretty well.

Christmas Eve came. Everyone was off to the church, in spite of their fears that that marauding beast was still somewhere around. What was it? A bear? A wolf? A wolverine? The tracks seemed more wolf-like than anything, but they always seemed to peter out, lost among the footprints of too many searchers.

Still, there was safety in numbers. Off to

church they went for the midnight service.

At the mill, life went on as usual. The millwheel kept turning. Joachim and Jean-Loup sat playing chess, drinking all the while.

Then, in the silence that followed the church bells ringing out at midnight, Joachim put down his glass and said, 'Listen!'

Jean-Loup shook his head. 'I can't hear anything.'

'That's the point! The mill wheel's stopped.'

It happened from time to time when a branch brought down by the river got caught up in the works.

'Come on!' said Joachim, grabbing his axe. 'Bring the lantern.'

Jean-Loup stood in the doorway, looking up at the bright, full moon. 'Why can't it wait till morning?'

'Because I say so! And I'm the boss.'

Joachim soon found what the problem was: a branch, as he had thought. 'Bring the light closer, so I can see what I'm doing.'

There was no answer but a low growl from above and behind him.

Looking back up the steps, he saw, not Jean-Loup, but a great, grey, wolf-like creature. There was something about its eyes that was almost human. Something strangely familiar.

'Jean-Loup!' roared Joachim. 'Help me! Where are you?'

The creature growled again, gathering itself. Then, it sprang.

Joachim lifted his axe and managed to get in a swing at the creature's left foreleg before it slammed into him, knocking him backwards. He hit the frozen ground and everything went black.

He woke to find himself tucked up in his own bed, with Jean-Loup bending over him, sponging his face with cold water.

Joachim was about to thank the young man for saving his life when he noticed a rough bandage tied round Jean-Loup's left forearm, the blood already seeping through.

'It was you!' he whispered. 'The beast that

attacked me. Jean-Loup – the loup-garou – the werewolf!'

Jean-Loup said nothing, only gave him that look with those feral eyes – the look that made you afraid to turn your back.

Joachim must have passed out again.

When he came round, Jean-Loup had gone.

I wish I could say old Joachim was a reformed character after that, but he was still just as foul-smelling, foul-mouthed and foul-tempered as before. At least he did talk to his neighbours more now. After all, he had a story to tell to anyone who'd listen. And there was something that always puzzled him, a question to which he still hadn't found an answer. 'I don't know why he let me live,' he'd say.

But if anyone suggested it might be because he'd been kind to the young man, 'Kind? Me?' he'd scoff. 'It's not in my nature!'

The Forest People
New Zealand

They are the patupaiarehe, the fair-skinned ones, who live deep in the forest, creatures of mist and shadow. Some say they are the people who were here before the Maori came. Some say they are nothing but a memory, yet they still have power. Power to steal away a man's shadow and what is a man without his shadow? Without his shadow he'll fade away and die.

The patupaiarehe were much on the young warrior's mind as he set up camp for himself that night. Somehow, he'd managed to get separated from the rest of the hunting party. He'd tried calling out and several times, in the distance, had thought he heard voices calling back, but they didn't sound like any voices he knew, nor any human voices at all, so in the end he kept quiet.

He'd find his way home easily enough come daylight.

So he rigged up a shelter beneath a cliff overhang and built a small fire, wishing he had some of the game they'd killed so he could cook himself some supper.

Still he could hear those strange voices in the distance, like something between human speech and birdsong.

He wrapped himself in his cloak, lay down and tried to sleep.

Soon they came, the patupaiarehe, whispering on the night wind, tumbling along on the evening mist, flickering through the shadows thrown by the fire.

He told himself they were just curious. What harm could they do him anyway, so long as he cast no shadow for them to steal?

So he curled himself up very small in his shelter under the cliff and pretended to be asleep.

Soon as they got bored, they'd go away.

He fancied he could feel their shadow-fingers stealing over him, light as moths in the dark.

His fingers strayed to the greenstone tiki he wore round his neck. A beautiful thing it was, so intricately carved, passed down from generation to generation, along with all the memories of his kinship group. Holding the tiki always made him feel braver.

The whispering voices grew louder, more insistent.

Was this what they wanted? The tiki? The most precious thing he owned?

It was heavy price to pay for trespassing on the territory of the patupaiarehe, but it seemed they'd be content with nothing less.

With a prayer for forgiveness to his

ancestors, he eased the tiki on its cord from round his neck. He withdrew a stick from the rough shelter he'd built and hooked the cord around it. Then carefully – very carefully, so as to cast no shadow – he held the stick out until the tiki caught the firelight.

At once, the patupaiarehe clustered round it like excited children – whispering, singing, leaping and dancing.

Gradually, their voices faded.

When the warrior dared to open his eyes again, it was morning. And there was the tiki, lying beside the ashes of the fire. Had it all been a dream? He picked up the tiki and held it so it caught the sunlight.

He looked down at his shadow. There it was, safe and sound. There was the shadow of his arm outstretched, his hand holding… nothing.

He looked again at the tiki, then back to where its shadow should have been, swinging the tiki back and forth.

Then he began to laugh. This was a story to tell his children and his grandchildren, along with all the other tales passed down with the tiki through the years. What good was the tiki itself, he'd ask them, to the people of mist and shadows? In the end, all they'd stolen was its shadow. And here was the tiki itself as proof. 'Hold it up to the light,' he'd say, 'and you'll see.'

The Goblin Pony
Britanny

'What are you doing, Grandmamma?' said Yann.

'What does it look like? I'm bolting the doors and fastening the window shutters to keep us safe from harm.'

'But it's Hallowe'en!' said Erwan. 'We were going out.'

'The only place to be on Hallowe'en,' their grandmother said wisely, 'is here indoors by the fire. Hallowe'en is the night when spirits walk and witches weave spells and dead men rise from their graves. And the wild hunt of the old gods rides the storm clouds in search of souls to carry off to the lost land of Lyonesse under the sea. So you stay here, my dears, and keep your old grandmother company. Cheer up! It won't be so bad. I've chestnuts to roast and toffee apples and a fresh batch of gingerbread warm from the oven.'

But, from their bedroom window, the boys could see the bonfire burning on top of the cliff, the figures dancing round it.

When they opened the window they could hear the sound of music from the village inn, where Yann knew the landlord's daughter, Barbara, would be waiting.

'Well, are you coming?' said Erwan.

'Try and stop me!' said Yann.

Out of the window they went, one after the other, climbing down the ivy-covered wall and they set off down the path towards the lane.

There – what a stroke of luck – stood a pony, quietly cropping the grass at the place where the path met the lane.

'Looks like Le Pen's pony's got out of his paddock again,' said Yann.

'We've no time to take him back now,' said Erwan. 'We'll miss half the fun.'

'We'll take him back in the morning,' said Yann. 'Meanwhile, he can give us a ride.'

So up they got and off they trotted till they came to the village inn, where Barbara, the landlord's daughter was waiting.

'Up you get!' said Yann.

'My! We're travelling in style tonight,' said Barbara. 'Isn't this Le Pen's pony?'

'Looks like it, doesn't it?' grinned Yann.

'Is there room up here for my sister Ann, too?'

'Of course there is!'

'There's plenty of room!'

'Up you get, Annie!'

Off they jogged again, back down the village street, until they met Pierrick and Padrig running hell for leather the other way.

'Help us!'

'Help us!'

'The widow Breck

says she'll have our guts for garters!'

'That's if old Markale doesn't catch us first!'

Since Pierrick and Padrig were known as the two local jokers and Hallowe'en is also known as Mischief Night, it was clear they'd been playing some practical joke that hadn't gone down too well.

'Up you get!' said Yann, digging his heels in the pony's ribs to try and make it go faster.

On trotted the pony at the same pace as before and not a bit put out, it seemed by the number of riders on his back. No, not even when they picked up two hitchhikers on the way, which made eight in all – Yann, Erwan, Barbara, Ann, Pierrick, Padrig and after them Little Eric and Fat Paol who'd been neither of them looking forward to the climb up to the clifftop.

Le Pen's pony, safe in his field, was surprised to see the mirror image of himself trotting past on the road below with so many riders on his back.

Well, rather him than me, he thought. And went back to cropping the grass.

It was when they reached the crossroads

that the trouble came. Instead of taking the path to the clifftop, the pony turned towards the sea. He picked up his pace, from a trot to a canter, then to a gallop, heading straight towards the seashore.

'Stop him!' cried Barbara.

'I can't!' yelled Yann. 'Jump, if you can!'

'We're going too fast!' shouted Erwan. 'We'll break our necks!'

'I'd jump if I could!' cried Fat Paol, 'But I seem to be stuck!'

'Me too!'

'Me too!'

Into the sea ran the goblin pony, with Yann, Erwan, Barbara, Ann, Pierrick, Padrig, Little Eric and Fat Paol stuck fast to his back, deeper and deeper until the waves covered them.

'I did warn them,' said Grandmamma, when those who'd watched from the clifftop came and told her the sad news. 'I warned them but they didn't listen. That's young people nowadays. They just don't listen. Ah, well, they do say the lost land of Lyonesse isn't such a bad place to end up. Would anyone like a piece of gingerbread?'

The Haunting
British Isles

For as long as she could remember, she'd dreamed the same dream. The dream was of a house. It was like no house she'd ever lived in and yet it felt like home. In her dreams she walked through its rooms, admired the pictures, fingered the books in the library, savoured the cooking smells in the kitchen, or wandered in the garden. Sometimes she just sat: enjoying the feeling of peace the house always gave her.

Sometimes it was daytime there, sometimes it was night. After a while it made no difference; she knew every stone of it so well that she could find her way by moonlight.

Sometimes the furnishings were different, the pictures and the ornaments, but always the layout of the rooms was the same. Sometimes, looking out at the garden, it seemed that the trees were taller now than when she'd first dreamed of this place. Just as she was, of course. It was as if she were living two separate lives, but the dream house was where she belonged.

When she told her sisters about it, all they said was, 'What's wrong with our house then?'

'Nothing,' she said.

'Don't you like it here?'

'I like it fine. It's just not...'

'Not what?

She shook her head. She couldn't explain it.

When she grew up and married, she never told her husband about the dreams she still had of her perfect house. She didn't want to hurt his feelings. All they could afford on his wages was a small flat in the centre of town.

At last he got offered promotion – that's if he didn't mind moving to the firm's head office across the water in England. He didn't mind a bit. The extra money he'd earn meant they'd be able to buy a house of their own.

House after house they looked at but none of them was just right, until they came to the very last one on the list.

As she got out of the taxi she gave a little cry.

'Are you all right?' said her husband. 'You've gone very pale all of a sudden.'

'Yes, yes,' she said. 'I'm fine.'

'Let's go and look inside, then,' he said.

The door was opened by the estate agent, who seemed surprised to see them.

'Are we too early?' said the husband. 'Were you expecting someone else?'

'No, no,' said the man. 'Quite the opposite. Let's start in the library, shall we?'

But she'd already found the right door and was running across the room to check the view from the window to see if it matched the one in her dream, which it did, exactly. She ran her fingers over the empty shelves, remembering the books that used to fill them.

The estate agent smiled to her husband, 'Perhaps your wife would like to lead us the rest of the way?'

And she did, through the dining room, the sitting room, the breakfast room and the kitchen, then down to the cellar and up to the bedrooms. Every single thing was as she remembered it from her dream.

'It's as if you've been here before,' said her husband.

'I have,' she said, 'in my dreams. But I never thought this house was real.'

'I never thought you were real,' said the estate agent. 'I've stayed in this house many times in the past. Sometimes I've seen you wandering through it, though I don't think you ever saw me. The last people to live here were afraid the place was haunted. But I don't think you will be troubled by ghosts. May I be the first to say, 'Welcome home'?'

Jacob and the Duppy
Jamaica

I t was late when Jacob set out for home that night. He'd had a good day at the market, sold all his produce, and so he decided to treat himself to a drink or two. And when a man's got money in his pocket and is in the mood to celebrate, he's never short of friends willing to lend a hand.

It must have been gone midnight when the bar owner's wife finally turned them out so she could get a bit of shuteye.

Jacob went back to where he'd left the cart (the donkey patiently waiting all this time), climbed up on the driver's seat, and they set off for home.

What with the gentle swaying of the cart and the quiet rumble of the wheels on the empty road, it wasn't long before Jacob was as sound asleep as a baby rocked in its cradle.

The donkey plodded on. She knew the way as well as he did: probably better, since she always did the full stretch with her eyes wide open.

Suddenly, she stopped. So suddenly that Jacob nearly toppled clean off the cart.

'What's the matter?' he mumbled. 'Are we home already?' Then, seeing nothing but darkness all around, 'Come on! Stop playing games. Let's get on home.'

The donkey didn't budge.

Then, peering deeper into the dark, he saw what was holding them up. A man was standing there, slap-bang in the middle of the road.

'Lost your way in the dark?' said Jacob.

The man didn't answer.

'Do you want a lift?'

Still no answer.

'I can take you as far as my place. That's a mile or so down the road. If that's any help to you...'

Already the man was climbing up beside him.

'Off we go, then! Soon be there.' That's if he could get the donkey moving again. She took a deal of persuading – and threatening – before she'd shift from that spot.

'Can't think what's got into her tonight,' said Jacob. 'She's not usually like this.'

The stranger said nothing, not one word. Not even when it started raining. Pouring down it was, like someone up there was tipping it out of a bucket. The stranger just sat there, didn't even turn up his collar to stop the drips from his hat going down his neck.

It was still raining when they got to the

house. Jacob jumped down from the cart, got the donkey under cover, and then ran for the porch.

He looked back and saw the stranger still sitting on the cart.

He didn't much care for the guy, but he couldn't just leave him, so, 'Come on!' he yelled. 'Come up here on the porch. You can wait here for the rain to stop.'

The stranger got down and walked over – no hurry – though he must be soaked through by now. The rain was running off him, forming puddles on the porch.

'Better get out of those wet clothes,' said Jacob.

The stranger nodded. Slowly he took off his broad-brimmed hat, his long coat, his boots and his trousers, till he was standing in his long white shirt.

Then, at last, he spoke. The words came out slowly, as if talking was something he'd learned to do long ago and he was having a hard time remembering the trick of it. 'Now you've got to help me,' he said.

'Help you?' said Jacob.

'Take out the pins at the back.'

'What pins?'

'The shroud pins.'

Finally, Jacob knew why the donkey had been so spooked when she saw the stranger standing in the road and why she'd been so reluctant to pull the cart with him on it. This was no living man. This was a duppy, risen from the grave!

Seeing the look on Jacob's face, the duppy grinned. Then it began to laugh. A deep down belly laugh, it was. The duppy laughed and laughed, till it was shaking all over, the way things seem to shake when you look through a heat haze on a summer's day.

Gradually, Jacob realised he was actually looking through it. The duppy was slowly fading. Fading clean away, along with the sound of its laughter. Last to go was the grin.

That grin of the duppy's is something Jacob will never forget. It's the reason he always makes sure these days to be home by nightfall. Even then, he can't be sure it's not going to come back and haunt him in his dreams.

The Selkie's Revenge
Scotland

There was a crofter living on the west coast of Scotland. His wife had died, leaving him with a baby girl to bring up, so now he toiled, day after day, all alone. Growing vegetables on the poor little scrap of land attached to the croft. Spreading his nets along the seashore in the hope of catching enough fish to make a trip to the market worthwhile.

Life would have been a bit easier if the

seals hadn't kept helping themselves. Time and again he came down to find a great hole in his net and not so much as a fish or two left for his own supper.

It made him angry. It made him wild. When he found a seal pup caught in the net, he didn't think twice, he just knocked it on the head.

He felt bad about it a moment after, when he saw the pup was dead, for he was not a violent man. He felt worse still when he looked up and saw another seal with its head poking out of the water, watching him with big sad eyes.

'It looked so like a human mother grieving,' he told the market women the next day, 'it put me in mind of the stories my grandmother used to tell of the seal people – the selkies.'

'You're turning fanciful,' the market women said, 'and no wonder – living alone on the croft with only a toddler for company.'

'Still, I know I never should have done such a thing. I don't know what came over me.'

'If you're not careful, you'll be turning

into a grumpy old man before your time,' the women said. 'What you both need is a woman about the place. Someone to come in each day and mind the child and the house, so that you can take the boat out the way you used to. You'd easily be able to pay her wages from what you made selling the extra fish.'

'Maybe,' he nodded. 'I'll think about it.'

A knock came at the door the very next morning. It seemed that the market women had been busy spreading the word, not giving him a chance to think about the idea for long enough to say no.

A young woman stood there. Big brown eyes, she had, and long dark hair plastered close to her head by the soft rain that was falling, though she didn't seem to mind it.

He had the strangest feeling that they'd met before, though for the life of him he couldn't say where or when.

'I heard you were looking for some help around the house,' she said, smiling past him at the little girl.

The little girl smiled back and the crofter

felt a pang of sadness. How long was it since his daughter had smiled at him that way? It was true what the market women said. He had been turning into a grumpy, unlovable old man without even knowing it.

So it was settled. The woman (whose name, she told him, was Mairi) would come early each day except Sunday and leave in the evening after dinner.

It was good to pick up his old life again. To put out to sea, feel the wind in his hair and taste the salt spray. To come home from market with money in his pocket, knowing there'd be a fire going and dinner ready on the table. Sometimes, he'd hear Mairi singing to the child as he worked the vegetable patch. Strange, haunting songs they were, such as he'd never heard before.

Sometimes, coming into the house, he'd find her and the little girl with their heads together, whispering secrets.

Other times they'd be gone all day, down to the shore as like as not.

'Mairi's teaching me to swim,' the little girl

said, her
eyes shining.

'She loves the
water,' said Mairi.

And he felt again that pang of sadness, a feeling that, little by little, his child was being stolen away from him. Even when Mairi wasn't there, the child would say 'Mairi did this,' and 'Mairi said that.' Whenever she said 'we', she meant Mairi and her. No room for him. No need.

He fell to wondering: what did he know about this woman, apart from her name?

Where did she go each night and on Sundays? Not to the kirk, for he never saw her there. Nor would any of the market women own up to having sent her to him. 'Word gets around,' they said, shrugging off his questions. 'Of course the child's fond of her. You're never there. Why don't you all do something together for a change, the three of you? Take them out in your boat, why don't you?'

The next fine day, that's what he did. Instead of taking the boat out alone, he got Mairi to pack up a picnic lunch for three. 'Today,' he said, 'you two are coming with me.'

So Mairi and the little girl climbed into the boat and the crofter pushed it off and jumped in after them and started to row.

As they pulled away from the shore, he looked at them sitting at the stern of the boat, arms round each other, heads together, whispering secrets.

Suddenly he burst out, 'What is it you want from us, woman? Are you trying to take my daughter from me?'

'Why not?' hissed the selkie woman. He knew now where he'd seen her before, knew her by her big brown eyes and her sleek black hair, now when it was too late. 'Why not? Since it was you that took my child from me?'

With that, she wrapped her arms around the child and flipped herself backwards. Over the side of the boat they fell and into the water.

He watched and watched and at last he saw, far out and heading for the open sea, two seal heads break the surface.

Then they were gone.

Often and often after that day he would stand on the shore and watch for the seals. And sometimes they came and sometimes there were none. But one seal looks much like another, so he had no way of knowing whether any one of them was his lost daughter. Or whether she'd drowned fathoms deep on the last day he saw her and was lost forever.

That was the worst thing of all. Not knowing.

As Cold as Clay
USA

She was a wealthy rancher's daughter and he was nothing but a lowly cowhand. Oh, but he had the bluest eyes you ever did see, hair the colour of honey and a smile that could light up the dullest day.

To cut a long story short, they were soon head over ears in love with each other. Nothing her ma and pa could do about it.

Oh no? Only send her away to stay with her aunt and uncle in the city, that's what they did.

(Well, the young man was a good worker, so no way were they going to part with him.)

She pined for him and she wrote to him, but he never wrote back, most likely because someone was making sure he never got the letters. Still, she knew he was pining too. So she wasn't at all surprised when she looked out of her window late one evening and saw him there, riding the best horse from her father's stable.

'Come quickly,' he said.

'What is it?" she said.

'You must come home.'

'Is something wrong at home? Is my father sick? Or is it my mother?'

'Just come,' he said. 'Come now.'

So down she crept, through the sleeping house and climbed up behind him and off they went, like the wind, on her father's finest horse, her with her arms around his waist.

Through the silent city streets they galloped and out into the country, across the wide grassy plain. Not a mouse stirring, it seemed, not a night bird or a bat to be seen flitting across the vast, starry sky.

There was just the two of them, together under the moon and the stars, and it felt good. Except that with the two of them cuddling up like that, there should have been some warmth between them, but, 'You're cold,' she said. 'As cold as clay.'

'I'm not,' he said. 'Feel my forehead. I'm burning up. The sweat's running into my eyes.'

She felt his forehead and he was burning up. So she tied her handkerchief round his head to stop the sweat running into his eyes.

On they rode, and on again through that thick, dark night, till they came to her father's house.

She slipped down from the horse and knocked at the door and her father opened it. 'What are you doing here?' he said. 'And how did you get here?'

'Why,' she said, 'didn't you send...?' Then she stopped. The horse and her lover were both gone.

Of course, he'd be in the stable, rubbing down the horse after that ride they'd had.

She ran to the stable and there was the horse, sweating and shivering, the saddle still on his back.

She turned to her father, who had followed her. 'Where is he?' she said.

Her father knew at once who she meant. Sadly, he shook his head. 'I'm sorry,' he said. 'He took sick right after you left. We did everything we could and the doctor said there was every chance he'd pull through. But then, this evening…'

'Where is he?' she said again.

'It's this way.'

He led her through the house to the room where the young man lay, in the bed he'd never left for three weeks past. She saw him lying there, stone dead, and round his head was that handkerchief of hers she'd tied with her own two hands not an hour before.

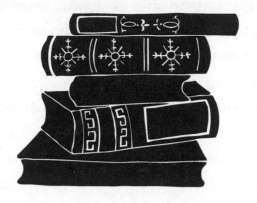

The Ghost in the Library
China

W hy the maidservant's ghost chose to haunt the library was something that would never be known. She hadn't left a note. How could she? She couldn't write. She couldn't read either.

Maybe that was it. Maybe haunting the library was the best revenge she could think of for having to dust all those stupid books, day after dreary day.

Now she haunted the library, night after

night, with terrible moans and howls and in a shape so fearsome, so it was said, that old man Chu gave orders that nobody was to use the library after dark.

'But I'm a student, uncle,' said Chang. 'I do all my best thinking at night. How am I supposed to know at sundown what books I'm going need at two o'clock in the morning?'

'You can take as many books as you like up to your room,' the old man said. 'The library will be locked at sunset.'

'That's stupid! Even if I believed in ghosts, what harm can a ghost do me anyway?'

'Rules are rules. It's for your own good.'

As to what happened later that evening, we must take Chang's word for it that it happened by accident. He was in the library, choosing a pile of books to take up to his room, when a particular book caught his eye and he settled down to read it in a corner that just happened to be out of sight of anyone standing at the door. Then, maybe the book turned out not to be not quite so interesting as he'd first thought. Or maybe it was the fact that he'd just had dinner and Uncle Chu's cook was a very good cook. 'I must have dozed off for a minute,' said Chang. 'Next thing I knew was the sound of the key turning in the lock and footsteps moving away before I could cry out.'

So he settled down to sleep again, his studies forgotten (it had been a very good dinner) until he was woken by a blood-curdling howl.

He opened his eyes and there was the ghost, moaning and groaning, with a wolf-like howl thrown in from time to time, fit to wake the dead.

Chang lay watching her until she ran out of breath (or whatever ghosts need to keep them going, since ghosts don't actually breathe).

'Is that it?' he said. 'Is that all you can do? I was told you were really scary.'

The ghost frowned. 'I can be really scary if I want,' she said.

'Go on, then.'

She stretched herself out, till her head was just below the roof beams and her toes were still touching the floor. Her eyes bulged and her tongue lolled out halfway down her chest.

'Not bad,' said Chang. 'But not scary enough. What else can you do?'

The ghost glared. She shrank back to normal size. Her head started spinning round and round. Faster and faster it spun, till it lifted clean off her shoulders. She held it up, spinning, on the tip of one finger.

'I can do that with a football,' said Chang. 'Do you fancy a game?'

The ghost put her head back on. She opened her mouth wide, wide, wide.

Chang covered his ears, expecting a scream, but what came out was a blast of ice-cold air, which gathered itself into a whirlwind.

Curtains and carpets, dust and loose papers, books, cushions, anything not nailed down, were all swept up in a dizzy merry-go-round.

Chang himself had to hang on to the nearest bookshelf to prevent being swept away.

The air was sucked out of his lungs. He could hardly breathe. Yet he still managed to force out the words, 'You're still… not… scaring me!'

The whirlwind died. The ghost had gone.

The next thing Chang knew, his uncle was

shaking him awake. 'My boy! My boy! Thank heavens you're still alive.'

'Of course I am,' said Chang.

'What about the ghost?'

'What ghost? Oh, that ghost. No problem. Do you think I could borrow the key of the library tonight, uncle? I don't want to get locked in again.'

That night, there sat Chang in the library, determined not to fall asleep this time (in spite of another very good dinner). He wanted to see the ghost appear and how she did it.

She came first in a cloud of evening mist, which darkened till it looked more like smoke. The smoke wreathed about, thicker in some places, thinner in others, till he could see a body forming, arms, legs, head and all.

And there she was!

'Hello,' said Chang.

'Oh, no!' she scowled. 'It's that stupid boy again!'

She stamped her foot, spun round three times and disappeared.

And was never seen again.

Goldenhair

Corsica

She was a merchant's daughter, not especially beautiful, apart from her long, golden hair. Everyone remarked on it when she was little. So soft, so fine, so fair! As she got older and young men started taking an interest, her mother always made sure it was tightly braided and pinned up in a modest coil on top of her head whenever she went out.

At home though, when she shook it out and sat in the garden combing it in the cool of the evening by the light of the setting sun, that hair was like a river of shimmering molten gold.

Count Rinaldo saw it as he was riding by on his way home from terrorizing a few of his peasant farmers and decided at once to marry her.

Her father was delighted. 'Think of the business he'll bring me!'

Her mother was over the moon. 'To think of hob-nobbing with the nobility!'

'But he's horrible!' cried Goldenhair. 'He's mean and cruel and miserly. Even his dog's afraid of him!'

All of which was true. On top of that, she was in love with Joseph, who was nothing but a common soldier.

Marry a common soldier? Out of the question! Maybe if he rose to be an officer, they'd consider it.

'But I love him!' sobbed Goldenhair.

'What's love got to do with it?' sniffed her mother. 'Do you think I married your father for love?'

'Well, I won't marry anyone else,' said Goldenhair. 'And certainly not Count Rinaldo! If it's my hair he wants, I'll cut it off now, this minute, and you can box it up with a pretty bow on top and send it to him.'

'Now you're just being silly,' said her mother.

Count Rinaldo was used to getting his own way. Step one of his plan was to get rid of his rival. He lay in wait for Joseph one dark night, but things didn't go quite as he expected. At the end of a short, sharp fight, it was Count Rinaldo who lay dying in a pool of blood, so he never got the chance to move on to step two.

Poor Joseph, meanwhile, having killed a nobleman, even if it was in self-defence, had to flee for his life.

'I'll come back for you when all the fuss dies down,' he promised Goldenhair. 'As soon as I've earned my promotion. After all, the emperor himself began as a humble corporal.'

So off he went and she waited and waited for him to come back again.

Then, one day in the market, a small boy

pressed a scrap of paper into her hand.

It was a note from Joseph. 'Great news! I have my promotion. Soon I'll be home again.'

Goldenhair ran all the way home. 'Mother! Father! Joseph's an officer now. Soon he'll be home and we can be married.'

Her parents still hummed and ha-ed – though they'd had no better offers for her since Count Rinaldo met his grisly end. So when an old woman who came to the door selling lavender whispered to her, 'He's coming for you tonight. Be ready,' she said nothing to her parents, only waited at her window till at last she saw a figure riding out of the darkness.

Down she went and climbed up behind him and off they went, like the wind. He spoke not one word till she asked him, 'Where are we going?'

'To hell!' answered Count Rinaldo. 'There, will you, nil you, you shall be my bride!'

'Never!' she screamed. 'Let me down! Let me go!'

The horse only galloped faster. Too fast for her even to think of jumping off, to end up nothing but a mess of blood and broken bones.

'Joseph! Where are you? Help me!' In despair she cried out her true lover's name.

Joseph, who'd been letting his horse amble towards the village while he slumbered in the saddle, dreaming of how it would be next day when he came to claim his bride, heard her cry from far off.

He spurred his horse to the top of the next hill and saw his love seated behind Count Rinaldo, her golden hair trailing in the wind.

Down the hill he rode to meet them, knowing he'd have but one chance to rescue Goldenhair, since no mortal horse could outpace Count Rinaldo's.

'Jump!' he cried. 'Trust me! I'll catch you.'

She would have jumped then, but Count Rinaldo caught her hair fast in his hand.

Then, Joseph drew his sword and with one blow sliced the hair clean through.

Count Rinaldo rode on, straight back to hell, with nothing but a handful of long golden hair by way of a souvenir, while its previous owner nestled safely in her true love's arms.

Goldenhair was Goldenhair no longer, since it never grew back quite the same.

In fact she looked quite ordinary.

Do you think that bothered Joseph? Not one bit!

The Werewolf's Bride
Spain

Don Antonio rode into town with a feather in his cap and money in his pocket. A fine young fellow, he was, in his scarlet coat and embroidered waistcoat. When word got around that he was in search of a wife, what a kerfuffle that caused!

True, he was a little on the stout side, but that only went to show that he liked to live well. A wife of his would never have to scrimp and save to buy a fine shawl, or a new lace mantilla to wear to church on Sundays.

Girls of all shapes and sizes set their caps at him, fair, dark and redhead, but Don Antonio only had eyes for Dona Ines. A widow, he was told, – so young, so sad, – and so beautiful!

And she seemed quite taken with him. He was already dreaming of wedding bells when he heard that she'd left town with another gentleman even stouter than he was – not to say downright fat – and old enough to be her father.

Don Antonio was broken-hearted.

A few days later she was back again. Alone.

'You don't seriously think I preferred him over you?' she said. 'We just went on a little sight-seeing trip, that's all.'

All went well for a while after that. He'd made up his mind to pop the question. Then she was off again, with another gentleman, even fatter than the last.

Don Antonio was devastated.

He did what he'd always done when he was unhappy. He ate more. He ate until the buttons on his waistcoat threatened to pop.

Then she came back again. Alone again and all smiles.

'You've put on weight,' she said, patting his tummy.

'I'm sorry,' he said. 'I was pining for you.'

'Don't be sorry. I like it. Did you really think I'd abandoned you? That man was a lawyer. I was hoping he'd help me claim my inheritance. Mine is a sad story, you see. When my husband died, he left all he owned to me, on condition I married his best friend. But I don't love this man! I could never love him. And he doesn't love me. All he wants is my money.'

'Marry me!' cried Don Antonio. 'Forget the money! I have more than enough for both of us.'

'You don't know this man,' sighed Dona Ines. 'He'd never let me rest if I hurt his pride so. I'd spend the rest of my life expecting a dagger in the back, or poison in my food. Perhaps, my darling, if you were to go to him, reason with him, man to man...'

'I will!' declared Don Antonio.

'And if he won't see reason,' added Dona

Ines, 'you must challenge him.'

'To a duel?'

'A duel to the death! Then I'll be rid of him, once and for all, and my husband's money will be mine... I mean ours!'

'What if I lose?'

'You won't lose.'

Don Antonio wished he could be as sure of that as she seemed to be. He'd never fought a duel in his life. On the other hand, if this fellow was as grasping as she said, there was a good chance he'd be able to buy him off.

Next morning, leaving the town in her carriage, he was in high hopes that by evening they'd be setting a date for the wedding. As the day wore on and the roads became rougher and the countryside wilder, he began to have his doubts. As the sun set, 'Is it much further?' he said.

'Not far now,' she answered.

So on they went and on again until at last, with the full moon shining overhead, they came to a house standing alone at the edge of a forest.

'It looks empty,' he said, hesitating. 'Are you sure he's at home?'

'Of course he is. He's expecting us. Have courage, my darling. Do this for me.'

'I will!' he said. 'You know I'd do anything for you.'

He let her take him by the hand and lead him up to the great front door. She pushed it and it opened at her touch.

'This way,' she said.

She led him through deserted corridors, finding her way in the almost pitch dark. Where were the servants, he wondered? Why were there no fires, no lights? Then, they were standing in a big, empty room. There, at least, there was a fire burning, whose flickering flames only made the shadows seem darker.

'Are you there, my darling?' whispered Dona Ines.

A soft, answering growl came out of the darkness.

'Patience, my darling. Patience!' She turned to Don Antonio. 'I have not been honest with you,' she said, 'and I am truly sorry, but when I tell you how it is, perhaps you will understand. I am not a widow. I married young and for love. It wasn't until the next full moon that I discovered that my husband was – is – a werewolf. He would have eaten me on the spot. Instead we came to an agreement. If I would bring him fresh, human meat – the plumper the better – at each full moon, then he would spare my life. So this is goodbye, Don Antonio.' Gently she kissed him on the lips. 'And thank you. Well,' she said, smiling, as she closed the door behind her, 'you did say you would do anything for me.'

The Hidden Hand
United States

Things were winding down after the Hallowe'en party, but Polly wasn't in a mood to go home yet and Cathy was her best friend, so she stayed on too. It was Tom's house, so he wasn't going anywhere. And Josh… well, Josh was always the last to leave any party.

They sat there, polishing off the last of the drinks, telling each other ghost stories, till they'd pretty much run out of those.

Then Tom said, 'Did you know that if you walk over a fresh grave on Hallowe'en night, the dead man inside will reach up and drag you under?'

Josh grinned. 'That dead man's got to be six feet down,' he said. 'His arms would have to be elastic.'

'I'm just telling you what I heard,' said Tom. 'You want to prove to us it's not true, you go ahead try it.'

'Maybe not tonight,' said Josh.

'I wouldn't do it,' said Cathy. 'Not if you paid me a million dollars.'

'I'd do it for nothing,' said Polly. 'Just to prove to you it's all hogwash. I'll go down to the graveyard right now. And to prove I really have stepped on a grave, I'll take this kitchen knife,' she said, 'and stick it in the earth right up to the handle. You can go find it in the morning.'

Off she went, down to the graveyard, and stepped, first one foot, then the other, onto the first fresh grave she came to. She bent down and stuck in the knife as hard and deep as she could.

She tried to stand up again and found she couldn't. There was something holding her down.

The others heard her scream. At first, they thought she was fooling. But the screaming went on and on. 'Help me! He's got me! I can't move! Help me, please!'

'I don't think she's fooling,' said Cathy.

'Me neither,' said Josh. 'What do you think we should do?'

'Maybe,' said Tom, 'we should go and help her?'

Then the screaming stopped.

'You think we should phone the police?' said Cathy.

'What'll we tell them?' said Josh. 'We think a dead man's got Polly? Dragged her down into his grave?'

'Maybe we should take a look first,' said Tom. 'How about if we all go together and take a peek over the graveyard wall.'

So that's what they did.

Peeping, one, two, three, over the graveyard wall they saw Polly, crouched on a newly covered grave, trembling and sobbing.

Tom pulled out the knife.

Josh helped her up.

Cathy found the tear Polly had made in her party dress when she stuck the knife into that newly covered grave.

She'd only pinned herself down when she stuck the knife in the ground – right through her dress!

River of Death
Morocco

Before there were angels in heaven or men and women walking the earth, in the time before time began, the djinni were born out of liquid fire. Mostly, these days, they live in the wild, lonely places and keep themselves to themselves. But just now and again they're apt to turn troublesome, maybe out of sheer boredom. Or perhaps to remind the rest of the world that they're still there.

So it was that the djinni who lived on the mountain above Azemour took it into his head one day to cut off the city's water supply by rolling a great boulder in front of the cave mouth where the river had its source. He said that if forty wise men could be found, brave enough to give their lives for the sake of the city, then the waters would flow again.

The sultan summoned his council of wise men – who happened to number exactly forty – and they all agreed that forty lives would be a small price to pay for the life of the city.

Then the excuses started coming.

'I would give my life gladly – but my daughter's getting married next month.'

'My wife is sick.'

'My son's causing problems – typical teenager!'

'There's a debt I must repay...'

'I have an epic

poem to finish. How can I deprive the world of my masterpiece?'

'There is an eclipse of the sun I must observe or all my research will have been for nothing.'

And so it went on, until only one was left, the philosopher Sidi Rahal. 'Who can read the mind of a djinni? Perhaps one life will satisfy him after all,' he said.

He didn't want to die, any more than the others did. As he walked up to the cave mouth he was just as afraid as they would have been, wondering what hideous death the djinni had in store.

Behind the boulder he could hear the pent-up waters roaring like a monster seeking for a way out.

He'd expected the djinni to be waiting for him, but there seemed to be no one about, apart from a wizened old man leaning on a wooden staff.

'Are you looking for the djinni?' he asked.

'Er, yes,' said Sidi Rahal.

'You've found him,' said the old man.

'You're the djinni?'

'That's me. I take it you're one of the forty wise men of the council. What happened to the others?'

'They... er... I'm afraid they were busy,' said Sidi Rahal.

'Not so busy they couldn't spare the time to watch you die,' observed the djinni.

Sidi Rahal looked back the way he'd come. There were the other thirty-nine wise men, carefully keeping their distance. 'Can we just get on with it?' he said.

'If that's what you want,' said the djinni.

'I'd much rather live,' said Sidi Rahal.

The djinni smiled. 'I'm sure you would, little man. But we can't always have what we want. Look at me. I asked for forty wise men willing to give their lives for the sake of the city. All I got was you. Ah well. Never mind.'

Then, the djinni began to change his shape. He grew taller, broader, stronger, greener. He roared and the sound was like thunder. Lightning flashed all around. He raised his great fist and Sidi Rahal closed his eyes, waiting for the fatal blow to strike.

He heard an ear-splitting crunch but felt nothing.

'Was that it?' he wondered. 'Am I dead?'

Cautiously, he opened his eyes and saw that the boulder holding the river back had been shattered into a thousand pieces, the djinni had vanished and he, Sidi Rahal, was still very much alive.

Not so the thirty-nine wise men who had only seconds to live. They thought they'd found a safe place to stand. It never crossed their minds that the djinni might change the course of the river until they saw the huge wave of water thundering down the mountainside towards them. They turned to flee, but there was nowhere to go, no time even to pray for mercy before, in a swirling, foaming torrent of water, they were all swept away.

So the djinni got his tribute of forty lives – all bar one. Why he'd been allowed to live was something Sidi Rahal would never know for sure. Who can read the mind of a djinni? Perhaps if the others had come willingly, the djinni would have spared them, too.

As it was, he'd asked for forty wise men brave enough to die for their city. All he got were fools and cowards. That, so they say, is why the river still takes its tribute of forty lives every year. A child playing too close to the water's edge, a young man taking a swim after a night out, a woman reaching after a piece of washing that's drifting away.

That's why its local name is the River of Death.

The Cold Lady
Japan

It was quite the worst time of year for a journey, but the old man insisted his business in the city couldn't wait till spring. So what was a good son to do, but go with him? As it turned out, they were lucky with the weather until they were part way home. Then, the blizzard struck. And what a blizzard! The wind howled in their ears like a thousand devils and the snow was an unbroken white curtain, swirling about them.

Still the young man would have pressed on as long as he could make out the road at his feet, but he could see his father (though he'd never admit it) could hardly put one foot in front of the other. So they took refuge in a cave on a lonely hillside and waited for the storm to blow itself out.

They had no water and nothing to eat. Worst of all, there was no way of getting a fire going. All they could do was huddle together for warmth.

At last, the old man stopped shivering and fell asleep. The young man, too, must have slept, because when he opened his eyes again, he saw that the storm had passed over. It was bright moonlight outside and there was someone moving about inside the cave. He saw a woman, dressed all in white. Her hair, too, was white as snow.

But her face in the moonlight was the face of a young girl.

The closer she came, the colder he felt, till he was colder than he'd ever been in his life before. She bent over his father, breathing a deathly cold over the old man as he slept. He saw the old man's last breath leave him, drawn up into the cold lady's mouth.

Then she turned towards him, the son. Strangely, he wasn't afraid, only faintly surprised. 'Is this it?' he wondered. 'Is this death? The end of all my hopes and dreams?'

'Such a pretty boy!' the cold lady murmured. 'So young! Too young to die yet.'

She was about to move away when she saw that his eyes were open, watching her.

'Swear to me,' she said, 'that you will never speak of me or of this night. Not to mother nor brother, nor sister, nor sweetheart, nor wedded wife, nor child, nor friend, nor foe, nor to any living creature that walks or crawls on land or swims in the sea or flies in the sky.'

'I swear,' he said. Then fell into a deep, dreamless sleep.

Next morning, he was found by some shepherds who were out searching for sheep lost in the storm. It took him some days after that to recover his strength and arrange for his father's funeral.

By the time he got home, he found his mother had taken on a new servant girl, Yuki.

'I think of her more as a friend,' said his mother.

'Her friend and her nurse,' Yuki told him quietly. 'You mother is sick, but I will do what I can to make her last days happy ones.'

So she did, moving quietly about the house, always there when she was needed but never in the way.

He got so used to having her around that, after his mother died, it seemed the natural step for them to marry.

And they were happy.

Seven children they had over the years. The children grew up and married in their turn. So now it was just the two of them, growing old together.

His hair was turning white. So too was Yuki's, though she still had the smooth, unlined face of a young girl.

So it was that one winter's evening, seeing her standing in the moonlight looking out at the snow falling on the garden, he was reminded of that night long ago.

'What are thinking?' she asked him.

'I was thinking of a dream I had once,' he said. 'At least, I think now it must have been a dream, though it seemed very real at the time. It was the night my father died.'

'Tell me about it,' she said quietly.

So he told her about the cave on the lonely hillside and the cold lady and the oath he'd sworn.

'Do you remember the words of that oath?' she said.

'Strangely, I do,' he said. 'Every word. It was never to speak of her or that night, not to mother, nor brother, nor sister, nor sweetheart, nor...'

'Nor wedded wife, nor child,' she said, 'nor friend, nor foe, nor to any living creature that walks or crawls on land or swims in the sea or flies in the sky. You broke your promise,' she said sadly.

Suddenly, the room was deathly cold.

'Such a pretty boy you were then,' she said. 'So young, that I took pity on you.'

She turned away, opened the window and stepped out into the garden.

He cried out, 'Take me with you! Don't leave me here alone!' but by the time he reached the window, there was nothing to see but the snow softly falling.

The Brownie under the Bridge
Scotland

Ever since he was a wee, small boy, Torquil had been afraid of the brownie that lived under the bridge. It began with his father, Torquil sitting up beside him every Wednesday, driving their pony cart to market. As they came to the bridge, his father would whip up the pony till she was going so fast it was a wonder she didn't go flying up into the sky, cart and all.

When Torquil asked him why, his father told him it was because of the brownie living there. 'If that brownie ever lays hands you,' he said, 'why then, you're finished. You'll never see your home or your kinfolk again.'

When he grew up and took over the farm, Torquil did as his father had done, going at top speed over the bridge, because the chances were that the brownie was still there. Brownies live a long time, so he'd been told, maybe two or three hundred years.

In time he married his childhood sweetheart, Jeannie, a sensible sort of a girl who didn't try to change his mind, since Torquil's fear of the brownie cut short their weekly trip to market by a good ten minutes.

Soon, she found she was expecting a baby. The weeks and months went by, until one evening she said to Torquil, 'I think the baby's coming. You must go and fetch the doctor.'

'What, now?' said Torquil, thinking of driving the trap over the brownie's bridge in the dark.

'Yes, now.'

'Can it not wait till morning?'

'This baby will be born long before morning. Off you go now and fetch the doctor.'

'Would it not be better if I stayed with you?'

'What do you know about delivering babies?'

'I don't like to leave you alone.'

'I won't be alone for long. The sooner you go, the sooner you'll be back.'

'What if I don't come back? What if the brownie…?'

'If you don't bother the brownie, it won't bother you. Please, Torquil, I'm begging you…'

At that moment, a knock came at the door.

Outside, stood a little old tinker woman. She was wrinkled and bent and smelt of fish and mouldering leaves, but Jeannie welcomed her in as if she'd been an angel sent from heaven.

The old woman had barely begun to speak, 'I wonder, could you spare me a bite to eat and if I could sleep in the stable…', when,

'Come in! Come in!' says Jeannie. 'There's a pot of stew on the stove and bread made fresh this morning. And a proper bed, too, for you to rest your weary bones this night, if you'll just keep me company while this man of mine goes for the doctor.'

'I'd be happy to,' the old woman beamed. 'Off you go now, lad – spit-spot!'

With the two women standing against him now, Torquil knew he'd no choice but to go, so he took the road at such a lick that he barely noticed the brownie's bridge till he was safely over it and knocking on the door of the doctor's house.

It wasn't till the doctor was fetching his little black bag that Torquil realised the pickle he was in. He'd got to drive the doctor back to the farm. Then, after the baby was born, he'd have to bring the doctor home again, and then drive back to the farm again, alone. Four times in one night he'd be driving over the brownie's bridge.

'No, no!' he whispered. 'I cannot do it!'

The doctor was very understanding when

he explained. 'No problem,' he said. 'I'll saddle up my own pony and ride behind you. Then there'll be no need for you to bring me home.'

But saddling up the doctor's pony took that little bit more time. And that pony could no more break into a gallop than fly to the moon.

By the time Torquil arrived back at the farm with the doctor riding behind him, he found Jeannie sitting up in bed with her newborn baby in her arms.

'Well, well,' said the doctor. 'It looks like you didn't need me after all.'

'Where's she gone?' said Torquil. 'The little old tinker woman who promised to stay till I came home again.'

'You mean the brownie woman?' Jeannie said smiling.

'The what? The who?'

Jeannie laughed. 'Poor Torquil! All these years you've been afraid of the brownie under the bridge and never stopped to wonder what it might look like! That one was the sweetest creature – and she's delivered more babies than you ever will, doctor, in a lifetime. No offence.'

'None taken,' the doctor said, smiling. 'Though if I were to live another couple of hundred years...'

The next day, Torquil took a basket of eggs and left them by the bridge on his way to market by way of a thank you. When he came back the basket was empty. Often after that he and his children after him – and his grandchildren and great-grandchildren too – would leave a little something now and then for the brownie, right up until the day they died, though none of them ever saw the brownie woman again.

Though brownies do live an awful long time. So it's quite possible she's living there still.

A Room Full of Spirits

Korea

There was once a boy who loved nothing more than to listen to stories. His father had an old servant who was a wonderful storyteller. Every night, he told the boy a new bedtime story. Every night, the stories whispered to him in his dreams.

The boy was also very selfish. 'These stories are mine,' he told the old servant. 'I don't want any of them to go beyond this room.'

That made the old man very sad. Like all

storytellers, he wanted to share the tales he had to tell with anyone who would listen.

But he was a servant. He had to do as the boy said. And, since all storytellers are, in a way, magicians, able to conjure whole worlds out of thin air, it wasn't a hard thing to do, to bind those stories so they never left the boy's room.

Time went by, the boy grew up and became too old for stories, but still those stories haunted his dreams.

Until the day came when he was to be married. The whole household gathered in the courtyard, forming up for the procession to the bride's house, where the wedding would take place.

All except the old storyteller. He was too old for all that junketing – the noise and bustle! Why couldn't people be married quietly any more, the way they used to do in the old days? He'd just creep in at the back when the ceremony began.

Meanwhile, he wandered round the empty house, enjoying the silence, until, passing the boy's room, he heard a whispering inside, of many voices. He eased open the door and stepped inside. The room seemed to be empty, but his head was suddenly filled with memories of stories he'd told long ago and almost forgotten. And with voices calling to him.

'Old man! Old man, we know you can hear us.'

'Please let us out. We want to go to the wedding too.'

'Have you forgotten us? You trapped us here. You are the only one with power to set us free.'

The old man smiled. 'Forgotten you?' he said. 'Of course not! How could I forget a single one of you? You are my children. But the young master commanded me...'

'Never mind what he said!'

'He's going away.'

'He doesn't need us any more.'

'Please, please, please! Set us free.'

The old man said. 'Go free, then, my children. Wander over the wide world, wherever you will.' It was like a weight lifting off his shoulders.

Oh, but then the whispering voices started

again, buzzing round his head like a swarm of angry bees.

'We're free!'

'Free!'

'Free at last!'

'Now to get our revenge on that selfish boy!'

'We'll teach him to keep us prisoner all these years!'

'I'm the story of the enchanted well. He's bound to be thirsty on such a hot day. If I position myself right beside the road, one sip of my water and he'll fall into a sleep from which...'

'What if he doesn't drink? Remember me? The story of the poisoned strawberries. One bite and he'll be turned into...'

'And if that doesn't work,' hissed another voice, 'I'll be lurking under the mat set down for him when he steps off his horse in the form of a poisonous snake.'

'Stop!' cried the old man. 'Stop! Come back!'

The story spirits were off and away down the road in pursuit of the young master, who wasn't a bad boy at heart.

What should he do? What could he do?

The wedding procession was well under way. Even if he could make it stop long enough to listen, warn them of the dangers, would anyone believe him?

Still, he had to try. His legs were aching and his heart was pounding by the time he caught up with the procession but he was not a minute too soon.

A servant was offering up a cup of water from a roadside well for the young man to drink. The old man dashed it to one side, seized the reins of the young man's horse and limped off again along the road.

Everyone was too surprised to do anything but follow.

The young man was still thirsty. When he spotted a field of strawberries, he called out to the old man to stop.

'Stop! Stop! A handful of sweet strawberries would quench my thirst even better than water.'

The old man didn't stop. For all the notice he took, he might as well have been struck stone deaf since breakfast time.

So they arrived safely at the bride's house,

where a ceremonial carpet had been laid down for the bridegroom to step onto.

Imagine everyone's surprise when the old man let go of the horse some distance away, rushed over to the carpet and whisked it up ... to reveal a snake rearing its poisonous head!

Luckily there were enough well-armed men around to make short work of the snake.

'You saved my life, old man,' the young man said. 'But how did you know the snake was there?'

So then the old man, having got his breath back, got his chance to explain about the snake, the well and the strawberries, and who could say what other dangers which might be lurking in the days to come.

'I was wrong, wasn't I?' the young man said, 'to try to keep these stories all to myself.'

The old man bowed his head. 'Stories are meant for sharing,' he said. 'We storytellers only borrow them for a while. The stories I told you when you were little, tell them to your children and your children's children. And they'll be content.'

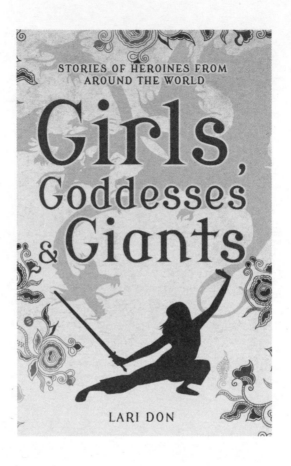

STORIES OF HEROINES FROM
AROUND THE WORLD

Girls,
Goddesses
& Giants

LARI DON

Lari Don's enthralling collection of folk tales
about heroines from all around the world.
These girls use their cleverness, courage or
kindness to win the day, beating wicked
witches, seven-headed dragons, shapeshifting
demons and greedy giants.

BLOOMSBURY

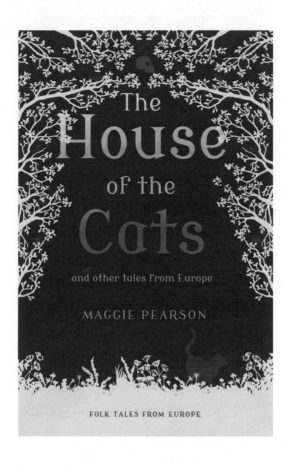

The House
of the
Cats

and other tales from Europe

MAGGIE PEARSON

FOLK TALES FROM EUROPE

A stunning collection of folk tales and
legends from all over Europe. Magical
to farcical, tender to terrifying, this
selection of often unusual and little
known stories from each state of the
European Union is a joy to read.

BLOOMSBURY

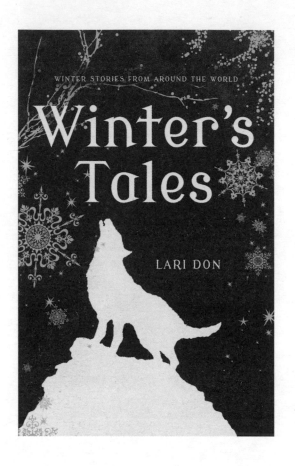

WINTER STORIES FROM AROUND THE WORLD

Winter's Tales

LARI DON

Lari Don's magical collection of folk tales about winter from all around the world. Find out how spiders invented tinsel, what happened when the spring girl beat the hag of winter, why eagle feathers made snow, and how a hero with hairy trousers used ice to kill a dragon.

BLOOMSBURY

STORIES OF ANIMAL SHAPESHIFTERS
FROM AROUND THE WORLD

Serpents & Werewolves

LARI DON

From the girl whose stepmother turns her into
a dragon to the werewolf's bride, and from the
god who becomes a fish to the girl who won't
kiss a frog, this fabulous collection is full of
shape shifters from all corners of the world.
Be careful; no one is quite who they seem!

BLOOMSBURY